The Island Child

OR MORE ABOUT WEENIE!!

● ●

Written by Monica Simmons MEd.
Photography by Wilson Baker
©1997

To my Grandmother
May all your days be days at the beach...

©text   ©photography
Today's Kids Publishers, Inc.   I. Wilson Baker Photography
4804 Calais Court   1094 Morrison Dr.
Marietta, GA 30067   Charleston, S.C. 29403
(770) 971-7511   (803) 577-0828

Design: Melinda Smith

My name is Tina. I live on an island. The island that I live on is called Hilton Head Island. It is not very big, but it is bigger than some of the South Carolina sea islands. I have always lived on Hilton Head Island.

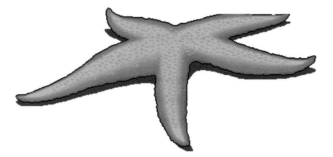

I go to SOUTH BEACH in the mornings to see the sun rise over the ocean. The sun lights up the sky so that it looks pink and blue. The ocean is fresh and the tide has come and gone. All of the footprints from the night before are washed away. My cat (his name is Weenie) comes with me to the beach. We go down to sit by the SAND DUNES in the COASTAL BREEZES.

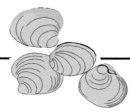

I can go out on the beach any time because I am an island child. Weenie can go out, too, since he is an ISLAND CAT. Skiddles, my little dog, cannot go out on the beach during the day. (Unless, of course, it is before Memorial Day or after Labor Day—that is the rule for dogs.) Skiddles must follow the rules about the beach, but she can go other places.

Some days, my friends come to visit, and we sit by the

pool near the beach. We drink SMOOTHIES that

the bartender at the TIKI HUT makes just for us.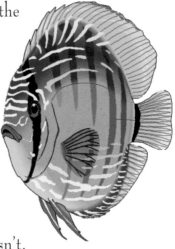

Weenie always comes with me. Sometimes, he chases

the SEAGULLS around the edge of the sand dunes

while we sit under the umbrella, and sometimes he doesn't.

It all depends on whether the wind blows his hair up in a furball, which makes

him cross. When he is cross, he likes to chase the birds away. It just seems to

make him feel better.

The water circles my island. There are lots of fishermen, boats, and beaches. Most days I wear only my bathing suit because I am on a boat. We often go crabbing or fishing. After we go fishing Weenie smells like fish because he always plays with the fish bait. I must wash him in the ocean. He hates being washed.

12

Weenie and I can swim whenever we want to. The average ocean temperature on Hilton Head Island is 69 degrees. Weenie thinks it is too cold to swim, and he sneezes when the waves come close. The average air temperature is 65 degrees. That is lower than the water temperature. So when we get out of the water, he likes it even less!

After a nice swim in the ocean, the sand sticks to the bottom of my feet, and to Weenie's feet. Weenie hates that. He takes a step, and shakes his foot. He takes another step, and shakes his foot again. Now, Weenie already knows this doesn't work because he tries it every time. All it does is make him cross and, of course, he looks absolutely ridiculous!! When I laugh, Weenie jumps and tries to shake all of his feet at the same time to try to show me that he's very smart. That's when he falls right on his chin. Now the sand is on his chin. Poor Weenie!

Hilton Head Island has 12 miles of beaches. When I go to the beach, I like to walk at the edge of the waves. I leave my shoes on the shore so they won't get wet. Weenie thinks it is a perfect opportunity to attack my shoes.

I like to build sand castles, fly kites, or ride my bike at the beach. Mostly though, I like to go SHELLING, ride the WAVE RUNNERS, or WATER SKI. It is fun to ski past the WIND SURFERS. They go so fast when the wind is high that it is hard to catch up with them. When I'm not on the beach, I like to play tennis and golf.

Other days, I go down to
Harbour Town to see the
MOTOR YACHTS. There
is a lighthouse there and I

climb to the top. Harbour
Town has lots of shops.
They sell ice cream, truffles,
books, toys, and all kinds of
gifts. There is a golf course
across the harbor. Beautiful flowers grow all year
round. Sometimes I see
famous golfers on the
EIGHTEENTH GREEN,
and sometimes it is just a
TOURIST hitting balls
into the water.

16

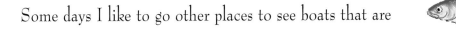

Some days I like to go other places to see boats that are

used for fishing. Some fishing boats go into the saltwater CREEKS and

INLETS. That is where Weenie sees the

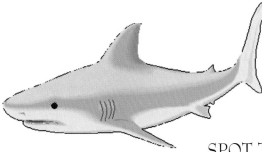

BOTTLENOSE DOLPHINS, EGRETS,

and PELICANS. The fishermen catch

SPOT TAIL BASS, BLUE CRAB, SHRIMP,

or FLOUNDER "close in."

The boats that go "way out" fish for KING MACKEREL, TARPON,

SPANISH MACKEREL, SNAPPER, and SHARKS.

Weenie and I like to fish too. Sometimes after we fish we

have a LOWCOUNTRY COOK OUT.

The fishing boats come in to all the marinas. The CAPTAINS know I like to play with the crabs. Weenie thinks the crabs smell bad and he tries to get away. Once one grabbed him right on the nose with its big pincher, and simply would not let go! Weenie was meowing but the crab hung on. Weenie never forgot. Now he just puts his nose in the air and is ever so careful when he sees a crab! Skiddles never remembers. She sniffs them and then she tries to play! Well, crabs don't particularly like to play with Skiddles. She ends up running away with a crab attached to her fur. It makes me giggle, but it only makes Weenie sneeze.

On certain days, I get to go to Pinckney

Island National Wildlife Refuge or Sea Pines

Forest Preserve to

see the ALLIGA-

TORS. The alliga-

tors are not tame, so

I don't feed them.

When the tide is

out I go SHELLING or BEACH

COMBING. I never take the shells or CORAL.

Sometimes I see SEA SPONGES

and SEAWEED. I see seashells

with creatures in them. My

grandmother told me that if I took the

treasures off the beach (and everyone else did too)

there would be no shells. So I leave the beach

just as I find it.

23

My grandmother used to come to see me and Weenie. Her name was Nanna.

She would take us to other islands. Across the sound from Hilton Head is

DAUFUSKIE ISLAND. Nanna often said it was the

most southern island in South Carolina. Daufuskie Island

has a lighthouse on HAIG POINT. People say it is haunt-

ed, but I'm not sure about that.

Nanna also took me to TYBEE ISLAND. Tybee Island

is on the coast of SAVANNAH.

I remember playing on the beaches and going shopping in Savannah. On some

days we rode on the riverboats. I liked to pretend

to be the daughter of General James Oglethorpe

when Savannah was founded. I would imagine the

COTTON WAREHOUSES along RIVER

STREET and the FREIGHTERS

from all around the world. Sometimes we would go down to the other

Georgia islands. St. Simons, and Sapelo Island have beautiful old

lighthouses, too. I loved to visit them with Nanna.

24

The island I remember the most is the one where

I spent my summers. It is a smaller island that is near

CHARLESTON, called SULLIVAN'S ISLAND.

Sullivan's Island is where my Nanna lived. She was born in

Charleston in 1901. She moved to Sullivan's Island when

she was a very little girl, and lived there the rest of her life.

She told me lots of stories about the South Carolina sea

islands. She told me stories about the sailors, the

LIGHTHOUSES, and the ships that came into

the harbor. She is gone now, but I remember everything.

She told me that early in the 1900's, ships came into the Charleston Harbor

from all over the world. Before that, there were naval stations all

across the coast of South Carolina. The coastal islands and

harbors were an important part of the Civil War, but that was

before Nanna was born. Even before that, troops had landed

in the South Carolina harbors during the Revolutionary War. Nanna

told those stories to me on the OCEAN PORCH of her house in the evenings.

Some of Nanna's best stories were the ones about the lighthouses. She told me

about her mother getting married on MORRIS ISLAND near the lighthouse.

That lighthouse was built in 1767 and was the first one in South Carolina.

Lighthouses were very important to the ships at sea. They showed where the land

was, and kept the ships from crashing into the coast at night or during storms.

Nanna's house was right next to the Sullivan's Island lighthouse.

My favorite story went like this: When Nanna was 13, there was a boy who

sailed in to port on a merchant cargo ship named the FREDERICK W. DAY.

He worked on the ship. His name was Sonny. Nanna would always look for him

when he came in. On September 17, 1914, the ship was bringing in bags of

cement from New York.

The ship went down in a tropical storm about 12 miles off the coast of Charleston, but Sonny was saved. Nanna said that an artificial reef formed when all that cement mixed with the sea water. After that, Sonny got a small boat of his own. He called his boat the Lady Luck. He used the boat to dive for sunken treasures from old pirate ships.

Sonny planned to ask Nanna to marry him as soon as he found a big treasure. Then, one night in a storm, his boat crashed against the jetties. It went down right outside of the inlet near Nanna's house. Nanna's father (his name was Sam Jenkins) found the pieces of Sonny's boat washed up onto the shore early the next morning. After that, Nanna said a mermaid came to sing on the rocks during the storms, to warn the ships away from the jetties.

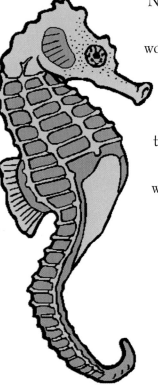

Nanna told me many stories about seeing the mermaid. I wondered if anyone besides Nanna had ever seen her. I always looked for her, but she was never there. Once I thought she was on the rocks, but when I looked harder, it was only the fog swirling up from the sea.

One evening around dusk, the sun was orange and pink and purple. It looked like a huge glowing pumpkin in the blue-gray sky. The weather had turned colder and summer was almost over. It was hurricane season and the weather forecasters were sending warnings that a storm was coming.

The storm blew in quickly, and Nanna was looking for me to tell me to come inside. But I was standing with Weenie at the shore, looking out at the sky. The sun was so bright and colorful, it looked like morning was coming. As the wind got stronger, it began to blow Weenie's fur so hard that he closed his eyes to keep out

the flying sand. Then the sky's colors got smoky. Weenie howled at me. He was ready to go into the warm house.

That is when I saw the mermaid. She was sitting on the jetties in the precise place where the Lady Luck had sunk.

Her back was to me, and she was singing a song that seemed to blend with the wind. She was sad, and she moved her arms as if to shoo away any boats that might approach the deadly rocks. Then she faded into the water. I could only see the small tip of her tail as she seemed to swim away. The wind began blowing big raindrops into my face and I couldn't see anything. Weenie howled and ran under Nanna's ocean porch.

As I ran toward Nanna's, I could hear that singing sound again. When I turned to look, it appeared as if the mermaid was pulling a boy out of the sea and placing him on the jetties. Then she faded away. The PALMETTOS and YUCCAS were bending in the strong wind. It blew me backwards as I tried to climb the ocean steps onto Nanna's porch. I looked back at the jetty to see if the boy was moving. That was when I fell and Weenie grabbed my dress and pulled me to the door. He wanted to be let in. When we got inside, Nanna was coming in from the street side of the house. She had been out looking for me in the Sullivan's Island Park. She was too happy to see me to scold me.

36

The only other time I saw the mermaid was when I went to Nanna's to close up her house. The family decided to leave her house just the way it was when she left. They covered up the furniture with sheets, and locked the wooden shutters.

On that day, I had gone outside. I was looking at the jetties as hard as I could. It was getting ready to rain, and I blinked back the tears because the strong wind was stinging my eyes. That was when I saw the mermaid again. She was with someone this time. Then I heard broken laughter in the wind. It was very young and happy. It sounded like my Nanna. The mermaid was singing the same way she did the day of the storm. I squinted hard to see who the other figure was. It looked like a boy. The rain started jabbing my eyes and the wind got stronger. When I looked again, I could only see the fog swirling around the jetties near where the Lady Luck had sunk into the ocean on that night almost 100 years ago.

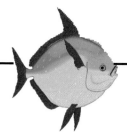

I go back to Nanna's to check on things, sometimes. I always go out by the lighthouse in front of the jetties. I sit there and remember Nanna. I think about the mermaid. Once in a while, in the mist of the early morning, I think I see them. The fog swirls around and the wind changes; and, I think that maybe I don't.

THE END

GLOSSARY

OF THE COAST AND LIFESTYLE OF THE SOUTH CAROLINA AND GEORGIA SEA ISLANDS

ALGAE—Water organisms eaten by fiddler crabs and other sea creatures.

ALLIGATOR—A large crawling reptile resembling a crocodile, but having a shorter, broader snout.

ANGEL OAK—(Quercus virginiana). Reported to be in excess of 1,400 years old. Angel Oak Park was opened to the public on September 23, 1991. The live oak species is found throughout the Lowcountry, especially on the sea islands. Older trees have wide, spreading canopies and massive limbs resting on the ground.

BEAUFORT—The second-oldest town in South Carolina, chartered in 1711. The site in 1514 of the second landing on the North American continent by Europeans.

BEST FRIEND OF CHARLESTON—The first steam locomotive in the U.S. to establish passenger service on a regularly scheduled basis.

BLUE CRAB—A bluish crustacean with a bony shell that is flattened.

BLUE HERON—A slate blue American species of heron having a long neck, long legs for wading, and a long, tapered bill.

BLUFFTON—Was incorporated as a town in 1852. It was first known as "May River" and later as "Kirks Bluff." Later the name was changed to Bluffton for the high banks on which it stands.

BOARDWALK—A planked bridge across the sand dunes from the inland area to the shore; it allows passage without disturbing the natural flora and fauna of the coast.

BOTTLENOSE DOLPHIN—Indigenous to the South Carolina sea islands and their surrounding waters. Les Parker has written an entire book about this dolphin.

CALIBOGUE SOUND—The stretch of water between Hilton Head and Daufuskie Island. Across the sound is the Intracoastal Waterway.

CAPE ROMAIN NATIONAL WILDLIFE REFUGE—64,000 acres of undeveloped wilderness 16 miles northeast of Charleston.

CAPERS ISLAND—A state wildlife refuge and undeveloped barrier island.

CAPTAIN—The master of a ship or boat.

CHARLESTON—The first established town in South Carolina, chartered in 1670. It was a bustling seaport in the 1820's and a port city of the Civil War.

CHARLESTON HARBOR—This includes Fort Sumter, Fort Johnson, Fort Moultrie, The meeting of the Cooper River, Ashley River, and Wando River to the northeast, and the Atlantic Ocean and the Intracoastal Waterway to the southwest. Also includes the area around Drum Island, Castle Pinckney, and the Battery.

CHARLESTON'S HIGH BATTERY—Historical area located in Charleston Harbor.

CHARTER BOAT—A fishing boat or other pleasure craft available for rent with a captain and crew.

CHELAE—The claws of the fiddler crab. In the male, one chela is much larger than the other. The male waves the large chela to threaten other males or to attract females.

COASTAL BREEZES—Winds that blow in from the open seas to cool the barrier islands and the shore area along the coast.

COBBLESTONE STREETS—Streets made from paving stone with convex upper surface.

COTTON GIN HOUSE—Outside building where the cotton gin, invented by Eli Whitney, was used to separate the cotton seeds from the cotton fiber.

COTTON PLANTATION—In the 18th and 19th centuries these were often 10,000-20,000 acres of farmed land.

COTTON WAREHOUSE—A large building used for storing harvests of cotton, common along River Street in Savannah in the 1800's.

CREEK—A small river emptying into a bay or inlet.

CYPRESS SWAMPS—Blackwater creeks that wind through the cypress and tupelo gum trees.

DAUFUSKIE ISLAND—South Carolina's southernmost sea island across Calibogue Sound from Harbour Town. Has been featured in Audubon and National Geographic magazines.

EGRET—Any of various herons with long plumes.

EIGHTEENTH GREEN—The last hole of the Harbour Town course, near the lighthouse.

FIDDLER CRAB—A group of small crabs that live along the temperate seacoasts.
These crabs burrow into sand and mud on beaches, salt marshes, and mangrove swamps. The waving of their chela (see CHELAE) resembles the movements of a person playing the violin, thus giving the fiddler crabs their name.

FIRST FLEET—This refers to the group of settlers who arrived from England in 1681.

FLOUNDER—A flat food fish.

FORMAL GARDENS—Flower gardens with winding walkways that graced the plantations of Colonial times.

FORT SUMTER—Located at the entrance to Charleston Harbor. The site of the beginning of the Civil War. The Fort experienced one of the longest sieges in modern warfare during that war. In two years an estimated 46,000 shells were fired at the Fort.

FREDERICK W. DAY—A cargo ship carrying cement that sunk off the coast of Charleston in a tropical storm on September 17, 1914. The cement formed an artificial reef approximately 200 feet long.

FREIGHTER—A cargo vessel.

GHOST CRAB—A pale, whitish, almost transparent sand crab indigenous to the coast of South Carolina.

HAIG POINT—The tip of Daufuskie Island where the lighthouse is built.

HARBORMASTER—The person in charge of safely directing ships into the harbor.

HARBOUR TOWN—The Eastern seaboard's best-known marina.

HARBOUR TOWN LIGHTHOUSE—Red and white striped landmark lighthouse that overlooks Calibogue Sound.

INLET—A recess in the shoreline.

ISLAND CAT—There are lots of island cats (just like Weenie!) at the Hilton Head Humane Society located on Spanish Wells Road.

JETTY—A pier built in water to deflect currents or to shelter an anchorage. A landing wharf.

JOGGLING BOARD—The joggle bench from the 1800's is about 10-16 feet long.

KING MACKEREL—A type of fish harvested for food.

LIGHTHOUSE—A tower displaying a warning or guiding light for ships at sea.

LOWCOUNTRY COOK OUT—See the recipe for this fabulous event in the recipe section.

MARSH FRONT—Low, wet land, a swamp.

MORGAN CREEK—A system of waterways behind the Isle of Palms.

MORRIS ISLAND—An island near Charleston. It is the site of the first lighthouse in South Carolina, built in 1767. It is one of 752 traditional lighthouses in the country. It was rebuilt in 1876 and marked the Charleston Harbor for nearly 200 years. It was originally built by decree of King George III.

OCEAN PORCH—A screened-in porch with ceiling fans that faces the ocean side of a beachfront house.

OLD EXCHANGE—Built in 1771 in Charleston Harbor, it became the social, political, and economic hub of the 18th-century port city. During the Revolution it was converted to a British prison.

PALMETTOS—Palm trees with fan-shaped leaves, indigenous to the South Carolina sea islands.

PECAN GROVES—In the 1900's, pecans were grown in large groves and picked by hand.

PELICAN—A large web-footed bird with a long bill and a pouch used to scoop fish for food.

PERIWINKLES—A small, edible snail that lives along rocky seashores. A trailing evergreen plant with blue flowers, a myrtle.

PORT CITY—A city along the coast with harbors used for shipping commerce.

REED—Tall, slender grasses with jointed stems that grow along the shore.

RICE PLANTATIONS—In the mid 1700's tidal swamps bordering the rivers were cleared and diked for rice cultivation. Today, many former rice fields are managed to provide valuable habitat for migratory and resident waterfowl.

RIVERBOAT—A floating craft used for hauling passengers or cargo from shore to shore.

RIVER STREET—The area along the port of Savannah used for commerce.

SAND DUNES—Deposits of sand by the wind around sea oats and other plant life that grows by the high tide mark. These are havens for many species of shore life, like the Ness Tern.

SAND SPURS—A weed of waste places with prickly fruit.

SAVANNAH—Georgia's port city. Settled by the English in 1733 under General Oglethorpe.

SEA ISLANDS—The islands dotting the coast, which stretch the 250 miles from the Carolinas to northern Florida.

SEA OATS—A large wheat-like plant that grows along the coastal dunes, holding the sand bars in place.

SEA SPONGES—A marine invertebrate that has an absorbent framework.

SEASHORE—The edge of the ocean where the waves break, leaving deposits of plant and animal life during low tide.

SEAWEED—A plant growing in the sea.

SHARK—An active, tough-skinned fish with triangular saw-edged teeth.

SHELLING / BEACH COMBING / TREASURE HUNTING—To search for shells or shellfish which have washed up on the shore in the tide.

SHEM CREEK—A salt marsh creek north of Charleston near Mt. Pleasant.

SHRIMP—A small saltwater crustacean resembling a crayfish.

SMOKEHOUSE—Often circular in shape, a place for smoking meat and game to preserve it.

SMOOTHIES—See Tina's recipe in Lowcountry Recipes section.

SNAPPER—A marine food fish resembling a bass.

SOUTH BEACH—Located inside Sea Pines Plantation—the southernmost tip of Hilton Head Island. It is the "toe" of the foot-shaped island.

SPANISH MACKEREL—An Atlantic food fish, green with blue bars and a silver underside.

SPOT TAIL BASS—Saltwater fish resembling a perch, a food fish.

SULLIVAN'S ISLAND—North of Charleston and adjacent to the Isle of Palms, Sullivan's Island was the key to the geographically shielded Charleston Harbor during the Revolutionary War. In 1962, the Sullivan's Island lighthouse assumed the role of the Morris Island lighthouse to mark the entrance to Charleston Harbor.

TARPON—A large silvery game fish of the Atlantic coast.

TIDAL MARSH—A marsh that is alternatively covered and left dry by the ebb and flow of the tide.

TIDE POOL—Depressed areas of the shore during low tide that fill with sea water, trapping fishes and sea creatures until the high tide washes them back into the sea.

TIKI HUT—A bamboo hut made with palmetto leaves with open sides to allow the ocean breezes through while still affording shade from the tropical sun.

TOURIST—According to the South Carolina Chamber of Commerce, 1.6 million tourists visit Hilton Head Island each year.

TYBEE ISLAND—A Georgia island off the coast of Savannah.

VERANDAH—An open porch or gallery, usually roofed—typical of the architecture of the 18th and 19th centuries.

WATER SKI / WAVE RUNNER / WIND SURFER—Modern day fun water activities.

WHARVES—A structure built on the shore for loading and unloading ships—mercantile warehouses.

YUCCAS—A plant of the lily family, abundant and indigenous to the Lowcountry.

LOWCOUNTRY RECIPES

These are easy ones!!

LOWCOUNTRY
COOK OUT

Corn on the cob

New potatoes

Smoked sausage

Clams

Oysters

Shrimp

Salt

Butter

Even Weenie can make this one! First put on a big pot of boiling water with some salt and butter in it. Once the water is boiling, put in the corn on the cob. Let the corn boil for 5-10 minutes, then add the new potatoes. Cook 5 more minutes, and add the sausage. (Weenie likes to play with the

sausages first, then, when he thinks they are properly dead, he puts them in the boil.) Five minutes later, add the clams. Five minutes later, add the oysters. Five minutes later, add the shrimp. Time to eat!

CORN IN THE HUSK

Sweet white corn cobs in the husk
Melted butter...lots of it!

Using a knife, cut off the first 2 inches of the corn at the top near the silk. Remove the outer layers of corn leaves down to the fresh green leaves. Drop whole ears into a pot of boiling water. When the water comes back to a boil, cover the pot. Simmer for 30 minutes. Remove the corn from the water, let cool, and shuck back the husk. Wrap a folded paper towel around the shucked husk, and you can use

46

it for a handle!

Dip the corn into a container of melted butter. YUM! YUM! (Recipe compliments of LowCountry Barbecue, Smyrna, Georgia—yes, there is a town named Smyrna!)

BOILED PEANUTS

2 gallons of water
5 lb. of green peanuts
1/2 cup salt

Combine water, salt, and peanuts in a stock pot. (Skiddles likes to break open some of the peanuts before cooking, and roll them across the floor to fully enjoy the event!) Bring water to a boil. Cover and cook for 3 hours. Sample for saltiness. If not salty enough, let stand in water for about 1 hour. A real Lowcountry snack! LowCountry Barbecue (Smyrna—right outside of Atlanta!—Georgia) says the best peanuts can be found between June and September.

FRUIT SMOOTHIES

2 fruits (Skiddles likes bananas!)
Red maraschino cherries (Weenie likes these cherries because they roll nicely!)
Vanilla ice cream (Tina likes lots of this!)
Pineapple juice
Chocolate

Put all the ingredients in the blender. Throw in all the chocolate you can find, any kind! Chocolate syrup, chocolate bars, Hershey kisses, and chocolate truffles blend up nicely! Eat it with a spoon, or use a big straw!!

References and Thanks to:

··

Beaufort County Historical Society

Billie Burn, Daufuskie Island, Historian

Charleston Chamber of Commerce

Charleston Historical Society

LowCountry Barbecue Catering, Inc., 2000 South Pioneer Dr., Smyrna (Atlanta), GA 30082,
(404) 799-8049   FAX (404) 799-1843

National Oceanic and Atmospheric Administration (NOAA)

National Climate Center, Asheville, N.C.

South Carolina Port Authority

U.S. Coast Guard